*Erin,
May ??
be yours!*

THE TRAVELER'S RIDDLE

Wayward Island Series Book 1

HOPE DANIELS
ALICIA DAWN

*Hope Daniels
Alicia Dawn*

This book is a work of fiction. The characters, incidents, and dialogue are drawn from the author's imagination and are not to be construed as real. Any resemblance to actual events or persons, living or dead, is entirely coincidental.

THE TRAVELER'S RIDDLE. Copyright 2021 ©

All rights reserved under International and Pan-American Copyright Conventions. By payment of the required fees, you have been granted the non-exclusive, non-transferable right to access and read the text of this e-book on-screen. No part of this text may be reproduced, transmitted, down-loaded, decompiled, reverse engineered, or stored in or introduced into any information storage and retrieval system, in any form or by any means, whether electronic or mechanical, now known or hereinafter invented, without the express written permission of Lavish Publishing, LLC.

First Edition

Wayward Island Series Book 1

2021 Lavish Publishing, LLC

All Rights Reserved

Published in the United States by Lavish Publishing, LLC, Midland, TX

Cover Design by: Aurelia Fray of Pretty AF Designs

Paperback Edition

ISBN: 978-1-64900-015-6

www.LavishPublishing.com

Contents

Prologue	1
1. THE TRAVELER	3
2. THE COTTAGE	11
3. THE INN	41
4. THE CASTLE	57
5. MORRIGAN	89
About the Authors	97
Also by HOPE DANIELS	101
Also from the Lavish Publishing family	103

Prologue

ONCE UPON A TIME, magical and humankind lived side by side.

Each governed by their own King, their own Queen, Lords and Ladies. Each with their own set of wonders to behold. Each with their own squabbles, wars. and malcontents.

As in any good story, there are Princesses and Princes beautiful for the eyes to behold. Some kind and benevolent while other souls rot in the morning sun.

This is but one of those stories.

This is a tale of a magical Prince and Princess, young and fresh to prove themselves worthy of their parents' admiration. Are they worth the lineage they inherit, or do they deserve to have it torn from their fingers as one might tear a scab away?

Only time can tell the true tale...

ONE

THE TRAVELER

ERIK STOOD at the large wooden table reading the missive his father handed him. He knew the importance of the documents. His father was rallying more soldiers for the battle to come. It was just one of the reasons he'd been called from his post. The other reason had to do with the line of succession. Civil War was nasty business to be sure, but when it pitted sister against sister it became downright evil with their people caught in the middle. For this reason alone, Erik regretted the loss of his brothers, though he would still be King one day. At least he still had his annoying little sister to call family, even if she was a pain in his arse.

"Erik, my son, I trust only you to travel in my name. The Lord Wellsley and his men are needed. You will assure he keeps his word. The man is known for selling his services to the one who can fill his coffers. Perhaps if you use the charm you use with the ladies, you will be able to get us his men."

"When do you want me to leave?" Erik asked, ignoring his father's comment about his prowess with women.

"Tomorrow morning. Arrangements have been made."

Erik wasn't surprised his father was putting so much faith in him. It wasn't the first time. The danger of opposing forces who would thwart any move they made was always at the forefront. He had the greatest chance to outwit any threat his aunt's opposing forces made. After all, he was a knight of the highest order and he was the Prince of the Silver Flame. "Don't let me down. son."

"Never," he promised. "I swear on this blade to accomplish all that you ask or give my life to the task."

"Eoin, what are you having our son promise to do for you so soon after I just got him home?"

His mother's voice always brought a smile to Erik's face. Caoimhe, her given name, always sang to him and his siblings. sweet songs of making. His most treasured memories were when she taught him to create unique magic. Caoimhe loved him and Abigail beyond any mother figure he had ever known in his experience.

Even he knew how closed off the court society was. It had been an eye-opening experience to the greed and corruption that saturated it when he was away. No matter the politics, his mother made sure joy and laughter were a part of every day.

"It's just a small errand. Nothing for you to worry your pretty head about."

"That is what you said when you sent him off to King Damek to train." His mother's spirited comment made Erik chuckle.

"'Tis nothing we haven't already discussed in the late hours between the sheets, my love," his father stated.

The sparks that passed between his parents were palpable, alive; almost a true being. The heat of their gazes tied his mother and father together; a golden cord from one heart to the other. Soulmates from this life to the next. He could only wish to find his own mate to answer his heart's call. Many years down the road, of course. He still enjoyed his bachelor life.

"Young man, you will be safe and take all precautions. Most importantly, there will be no tupping along the way." Caoimhe demanded.

If his mother knew how he spent his free time, it would put more white hair on the edges of her brow than his sister had currently placed.

"Leave the man alone, Caoimhe. He is the same age as I when I first laid eyes upon you, as I recall. I believe you took every opportunity to find yourself alone with me."

"Listen to this drivel. I'll not stand here while you fill our son's head with lies when it was you who followed me like a lost lamb."

"Aye, and I'll follow you always." His father made a grab for his mother's behind.

"This is the perfect time to excuse myself," Erik stated. The last thing he wanted was to be privy to his parents' tupping while he pretended to be looking over maps again.

"Now look, woman, you've chased off…"

"I've not chased off our son. Erik, stay. Finish your planning. His Royal Highness will throw a temper tantrum if you leave now." His mother's laughter always lightened the mood.

"Aye," he said. "We wouldn't want the King to be dismayed."

"I'll leave you boys to plan your trip. Be safe, my son. Husband, you and I shall finish our discussion privately at a later time."

"That we will, wife."

Erik and his father stood as Caiomhe left the room.

She may have entered silently, but her retreat was anything but quiet.

"You will leave in the morning. Take Thomas with you to relay messages." His father stated, once again getting back to the business at hand.

"I will do as needed to take care of the matter," he assured his father. Already his mind was on the mission ahead. He'd have his page gather what he and Thomas would need and prepare their horses. "We shall leave at first light."

The private quarters were too quiet. She knew better than to have a tryst this late in the day. However, Erik's squire was quite handsome, virile, and held a magical quality about him which intrigued her. Tying her riotous curls back with a ribbon, Abigail dressed quickly before her mother could come find her. With her brother in residence, it wouldn't be long before her father sent him around the lands to collect the rent, or on some other errand. She planned to go with him whether he deemed it appropriate or not. She'd had a vision of the importance of her attendance on her brother's travels; though he would call it the dream of a silly female, she knew differently.

Gran had taught them both to recognize their powers. Erik tended to ignore his; typical male relying on his physical prowess rather than all of the gifts the Goddess gave. Abigail hid quickly at the approach of the sumptuous silk skirts brushing together. Her mother. A confrontation she needed to avoid. Outside of her father's study, she took up a position to eavesdrop, but of course that isn't what she would call it. Not at all. Abby would swear she was listening outside of the door for one purpose and one purpose only--to preserve her brother's life.

As Erik and her father spoke, a plan formed in her head. One which placed a cat, who ate the canary smile upon her face. A secret smile for squire Thomas to enjoy before passion took hold of them. Until, mayhap, he realized he'd been left behind and she had taken his place at Erik's side. Unfortunately, it may mean she may never have the pleasure of his company in her bed again. A crying shame too. The man was very talented with his tongue.

Engrossed in her plan, Abigail did not hear the movement from inside the room until the door handle began to turn. She gasped before rushing quickly down the hall toward the kitchens. where the smell of freshly baked bread called to her. Besides, she had to concoct her potions, prepare her own bag and after Erik spoke with Thomas, she would charm him with her body, ply him with food and take his place beside her brother on this adventure.

With so little time, Abigail took a small loaf of bread, a bit of cheese and left out the servant's entrance. She had herbs to gather and a male to seduce all before nightfall. Then her true work will begin. She passed a low window and noticed her reflection giving a frown. Truly she would hate the loss of her long red locks, but it must be done to ensure her brother's success. The truth of it burned deep in her soul. If she did not follow Erik, he would die. She would not allow another brother to leave her. Not while she had the power to stop it.

TWO

THE COTTAGE

ERIK ROSE BEFORE THE SUN. The sooner he left, the sooner he'd be able to be home again. He'd forgotten how much being around his family helped him center internally. He didn't practice the magic like his baby sister did, nor did he feel it necessary. Brain and brawn would win this battle to come. The women could handle the potions and spells, it was what they were good at. Erik's satchel laid on his chest, empty of essentials he was going to need for the trip. A pox on his squire. The boy should have taken care of it last night before he'd gone to bed. Frustrated, he stuffed his bag with what he would need, slung it over his shoulder and headed towards the kitchen to grab some food. The kitchen cooks always had leftovers from the night before. Not disappointed, he grabbed a loaf of bread, probably intended for breakfast. Wrapping it and a chunk of cheese in cloth he stuffed it into his satchel, but not before taking a bite to quiet the rumbling of his belly. Voices coming down the hall had him ducking out the back door. The one thing he didn't want was to be scolded by the cook as he had been as a child. Fond memories to be sure, but he didn't have time to reminisce.

Though relatively somber, the castle grounds began the morning routine. The laundress filled the kettle with fresh water to boil. The fire was already burning brightly. Soldiers nodded their heads Erik's way, yet no one stopped to speak to him. Stable boys pushed carts of dung toward the wood so his mother would not have to smell the stench. To Erik, all these sounds and smells meant home and lifted his spirits. This errand his father wanted him to complete should be simple enough he thought as he entered the large wooden structure housing all the horses. To greet him, a mare pissed on the freshly washed wooden floor marking his boots with her scent. Whinnies and snorts welcomed him. and his own steed started knocking his hooves against the oak door as soon as he saw Erik heading his way.

"Good morning, boy." He rubbed the soft nose as it blew hot air across his face. "Are you ready for another adventure? Hmm?" Palming the sugar cubes, he'd swiped on his way out of the kitchen he fed them to Holok. "Now where is Thomas? He should have you saddled and ready to go." The lack of his squire's appearance put lines of frustration on his otherwise calm features. All due to the boy's impertinence. "Thomas, shake a leg." Eric hollered, knowing Thomas could hear his booming voice in the room he kept in the back of the stables. A long-drawn-out sigh left him after waiting a couple of minutes and getting no response. He wasn't going to wait around for the boy, Thomas could catch up with him. Eight minutes later, his steed was ready to go and there was a note on Thomas's door stating he was going on without him, and to catch up or else.

"Thomas?" Abby whispered. Her call was met with soft snores making her smile. A good plan, a sated man and a well-made potion. She would crow if it wouldn't alert the household. No one needed to know she was awake much earlier than normal. Not on this day. Not when the only persons who would see through her glamour would be her parents and her brother. Honestly, she would much rather stay in bed next to Thomas than chase her brother on his adventure.

Her father was correct, however, without a member of the royal family to assure that Lord Wellsley kept his word, the man would sell them out to the highest bidder. If only the Goddess were willing to strike that man down, but it was not her place to choose his fate. Mind now on the task at hand, she removed Thomas' hand from her breast and climbed from the bed.

"I'm sorry, love. Please forgive me when you wake," she whispered before kissing his cheek.

With a quick brush of her hair, a leather thong tying back her mane of curls, she stepped into Thomas' clothes. Though the shirt hung below her arse, she had combined two spells to shrink the clothes to fit. It worked like a charm.

"A charm. I am funny even when there is no one else awake in the room," she stated aloud.

Glamour finally in place, she left the palace via the kitchens. This time she left with her head held high, a satchel of food for her *trip* and headed for the stables with a quick step as Prince Erik had already filled his satchel and left Thomas, actually her, behind.

Thomas, when you crawl away from whomever you bedded last eve, get your arse on your horse and catch me up. Consider yourself discharged if you do not do so by midday.

Erik

When Abigail read the note, she rolled her eyes. It was a habit she seemed unable to break where her brother was concerned. Always moving in a forward motion, he rarely took the time to see the world around him. Unless, of course, the world included beautiful breasts and a smile to match. Entering the stables, Abigail's horse whinnied seeing right through her spell. Tempted to reassure her mount, she smiled and pushed magic of love toward the mare rather than touch the beast. Instead, she found Mondis, Thomas' steed, snorting in his stall, saddled and ready to go. *Thank you, Erik.* Sure, that her brother was the reason she was able to mount the animal immediately. Abigail sent thanks to the Goddess and though the horse was skittish, she walked him out of the barn. Once they cleared the doors, she clicked her tongue, and he took off in a quick trot in the direction of Lord Wellsley's castle.

The clopping of the horse's hooves tipped her brother off; she was behind him, but Erik didn't look in her direction when he started talking.

"Next time I'll drag your hide out of your bed. I will not care if you are with a whore or not Thomas. Who was she this time? The pretty blonde upstairs maid or the laundress's daughter who lifts her skirts for anyone with a coin? With you, it had to be both to keep your lazy arse from getting up when I needed you. Don't think you'll be dipping your wick in every willing female on this journey. There'll be time for that when you get back home," Erik lowered his voice. "Oh, and if I catch you sniffing around my sister's skits, I'll make sure you never bed another woman again. Don't think I didn't miss the looks she gave you. Abby gives those looks to every male she thinks she can wrap around her little finger. Our father spoils her rotten because she's the baby. But I know one day a real man will teach her how a woman should behave and keep her barefoot and pregnant, so she stays out of trouble. She will be barefoot because of the earth mother she will become, but she will have a passel of kids hanging onto her ankles."

She opened her mouth to give him a scathing retort but stopped herself when she remembered she was supposed to be Thomas, not herself. "Aye, Milord. As will you, I am told. I hear many things while in the arms of the upstairs maid."

A real man indeed. Her brother wouldn't know about being a real man. A real man would let a woman have her lead and only reign her in when the danger proved too great. Danger to the kingdom, not to his ego. She'd not met many men who were strong enough in their manhood to not be threatened by a strong woman. A man like her father. Erik would need two strong lovers to tame him. She had seen it. A strong, soft, loving woman who would balance the violence that would soon erupt from within him. The why of it she did not know, only that it would come. He would also need a warrior to be able to take the anger from him.

"Bloody hell, Abigail! What are you playing at? Turn around right this moment and head back home," Erik snapped. Apparently, her spell wasn't as good as she thought it was. "This is no place for a woman, let alone a spoiled princess out for an adventure."

Her brother was many things but understanding of little sisters was not one of them. A farmer could have planted wheat in the depths of the furrows upon her brother's brows. His glare was nothing new. She received it many times and would receive it many more before their lives on this earth were finished.

"Why are you dressed in boys' clothes? Never mind, obviously mother doesn't keep you busy enough, so you have to poke your nose into things like usual." Erik interrogated. The fact he kept ranting in his brotherly way made her remove her glamour. After all, they were in the middle of nowhere with no one around. "I'm surprised you've kept your mouth closed this long without a snappy comeback, sister." Erik stopped and swung his horse around, so he was up close and in Abigail's space.

"Why would I speak, dear brother? I am, after all, only a lowly female." She held Mondis in place giving Erik the same droll stare he sent her way. "If I were to tell you Thomas was safely tucked in my chambers, you will be angered at me, not at the weakling of a man. If I say I am here to keep you out of trouble, you will laugh and place your haughty nose in the air and say I will be more trouble than I am worth. But I am here as the Goddesses emissary. Erik, and I will save you from yourself. I have lost too many brothers to their egos as it is." With her strong declaration, she urged Mondis to move around her brother before he could say another word. Let him chew on the truth for a moment or two while she added distance between herself and home.

"You are a pain in the arse. Always have been. Always will be. Put your glamour back up, who knows what's lurking in the woods. If you're supposed to save me then at least do a better job than you're doing now." Erik gigged his horse and galloped by his sister at a breakneck speed. The murderous look on his face made Abigail sigh. She'd always been good at pissing off her brothers. It looked like her job was done for the day. Abby would give him a couple hours to cool off before talking to him again, at least he wasn't forcing her to go home. Thank the Goddess for small favors.

Erik wouldn't admit to his sister she had a valid point, he'd never hear the end of it, and she needed to keep her spoiled bratty self in check. To say the least he wasn't none too happy she decided to insert herself into his business, even if she thought she could keep him out of trouble by protecting him by her girlish magic. He gave a snort of disdain, like he needed a female to protect him, he'd been trained by the best in hand-to-hand combat, and magic was second nature to him. He didn't depend on piddly little spells like his sister. Erik needed to tell his father Abigail needed to wed and soon. Maybe it would keep her out of mischief by taking care of a passel of kids.

Time seemed to pass quickly as Erik turned his thought to the journey ahead and what he needed to do. His horse kept a steady brutal pace, making it a hard ride for Abigail, since she wasn't used to it. It was going to be a three-day ride to reach the castle and he wouldn't waste time on keeping her comfortable. She wanted to be here, and damn me if she was going to learn it had been a bad decision on her part. By evening they came upon a clearing with a stream flowing nearby.

"We're stopping here for the night." Erik informed a saddle worn Abby. Crows cawed from nearby announcing their presence. He tried not to laugh at her disheveled appearance. She caught his smirking and sent him a nasty glare. "Gather some wood, while I water the horses."

"Fine, it isn't as if my arse hurts or anything," she

spat. He laughed at her wobbly legs when she dismounted.

"That there is what happens when you're on your back more than you are on your feet."

"Well then, brother, it is a good thing Holok has a sure foot and can run in the right direction while you are rubbing yourself off as no woman in her right mind would bed an arse like you."

"Whereas I do not flaunt my charms like a dock side doxy, my sexual exploits are none of your business."

"You are daft. Erik. The entire kingdom knows of your sexual exploits. Women and men. You are fooling no one. You are a lover, not a fighter. This is why I am here." Erik started laughing at his sister's statement.

"You're only here because I allowed it. When father finds out you won't be able to sit down for a week."

"I already feel as if I cannot sit for a week," she mumbled to his enjoyment. With reins in hand, he pulled her horse and his down to the water, hearing Abby's stumbling steps breaking twigs, trying to keep her balance when he removed her tenuous hold she had on her saddle.

Arse burning like fire, Abigail regretted following her brother this very moment. Gods knew how he tried her patience. Yet, she loved him and knew he loved her. Elsewise he would have sent her home immediately upon finding she had deceived him.

Her inner thighs screamed in pain when she walked bowlegged into the forest to find wood. You'd think after a night of lovemaking, they wouldn't hurt, but no, not with her brother riding like Cerberus was chasing them all day nipping at their heels. The trees provided a way to balance herself as she stooped to pick up wood. Abby felt drunk on mead weaving from one place to another.

She gasped. A vision flashed before her of blood, a fire, a raven, and her brother. "Erik," she shouted. Abigail retraced her steps as quickly as her aching body would allow her to move. They needed to leave this place and leave it now. As loathe as she was to get back into the saddle, their safety demanded they both do so in haste. Deep in her soul Abby *knew* Erik was in danger. It sickened her to think she may already be too late. Tears filled her eyes at the thought. She would not lose the only brother left to her. It would not only break her parent's hearts, but her own as well. Erik was everything to her. Inasmuch as they teased one another, harshly at times, Abigail could not imagine life without Erik's bossy ways, or the crinkle of the corner of his eyes when he smiled at her.

"Erik," she shouted once more. This time she reached their camping site in time to see him return with a strange older woman beside him. Abby knew immediately the woman was an evil practitioner. Abigail firmed the hold on her glamour while her mind began to race. How could she save them both? How could she save her brother from the vision she was shown?

"Thomas, you have come at the best of times. May I introduce Shona. She is a widow who lives in a nearby cottage."

With her eyes narrowed at how close Shona stood next to her brother, as the disguised page, Abigail bowed.

"Milady, merry meet."

"Blessed be, my child," the hag stated.

Abby fumed. The widow's wicked tant could be felt where she stood. How many other unsuspecting travelers did she lure with her web of deceit?

"Leave the firewood, Thomas. Shona has graciously offered us a place to stay for the night."

"What?" she asked incredulously.

"Aye, my cottage is small, but just along that path through the wood." The woman pointed a gnarly talon towards the place where there had not been a path before.

Gooseflesh rose along the back of Abigail's neck. Her opponent was formidable, but Gran had taught her well.

"How kind of you, milady," she choked out the words sending her brother a look wishing she could smite him where he stood, because of his stupid male member doing the thinking for him. All thoughts she had earlier wishing she hadn't come on this trip vanished like wisp of smoke. This is why he needed her on this journey. His cock would lead him to death's door before the sun went down. *I am going to have a talk with mum when we get back home. Erik needs a wife to keep him in line and his wick in check. A passel of children clinging to his legs wouldn't harm him either.*

"Shake a leg Thomas, before the sun sets." Mentally calling Erik every name in the book, Abigail stiffly walked over to her horse and swallowed a hiss of pain when she put her foot in the stirrup. Grabbing the pummel, she tried to pull herself up, but her body wasn't cooperating. It didn't help hearing the crone snicker from her position in front of Erik on his horse. After three failed attempts, her brother waved his hand and used magic to plant her in the saddle with the reins in her hands. This time Abby couldn't suppress the sound of moaning pain when her arse hit the leather.

The pain intense, "Shite," left her lips before she could stop it.

"What is that, Thomas?" Erik gave her a pointed look before urging his horse to begin walking.

"Nothing milord," Abigail stated quickly. "Just overwhelmed by this opportunity." Abby gave them a fake smile and followed. She ignored the flirting on the short jaunt down the path, if she did not, she might lose her last meal. The old crone was too enthralled by Erik's considerable charms to recognize a formidable opponent when faced with one. Abigail vowed to dispatch of this evil carrion before she could lay one wrinkle, dried lip upon Erik's cheek.

I don't know what you plan, crone, but I see through your shimmering spell to the decaying evil beneath. The older witch, not unlike her brother, seemed so sure of herself and her abilities. How could they not see what was in front of their very eyes? Gran had spoken many times of the power which radiated off Abigail's aura. Just as Gran told her how she needed to keep herself under control, her grandmother knew and saw things other witches did not. Her gran was a powerful witch indeed and became a teacher to those with more than one power, like herself. Sometimes Abby missed those lessons and wished for days gone by. Gran would talk of dark witches. Caiomhe would not. What Caiomhe did not understand was that Abby had already seen dark witches. Some from the safety of her gran's seeing bowl and some from behind her gran's protective veil. This one was no different. *Self-absorbed peacock.* She knew how to deal with peacocks. Praise their beautiful glory and offer them poisonous seeds. Oh, how she would love to poison the old witch before the woman could use her dark magic on her or Erik. The feel of her talisman hanging heavily between her breasts, caressing softly gave her comfort that she was on the right path. Too bad it didn't comfort her sore arse from riding the horse. Had she foreseen this part of the journey, she would have prepared better.

Abby's internal musing helped to pass the time. Before she knew it, they had come upon a small cottage in a meager clearing, which appeared to have seen better days. Keen eyes could feel no magics trying to disguise the grounds, or the gardens she could just see toward the back. The hag would not try to hide those essentials and many of the roots needed for evil spells could not be raised in the average garden bed. Yet something warned Abby to be wary.

"Thomas. Thomas," Erik shouted. The tone of his voice pulled Abby from her musings. "Our hostess has stated that her well is close to dry. You will have to water the horses at the stream behind the cottage." Her gaze followed as he pointed. Auburn brows scowled down at her brother. This charade of his was going a bit too far. It was all her opinion, of course. It didn't matter that she chose to start pretending to be Thomas in the first place. Erik didn't have to continue to play along when her bottom was on fire and it hurt to move let alone walk two horses to the river. Besides, she wouldn't be able to watch out for him while she was gone.

"Aye, milord," she acknowledged. "'Tis a good thing you've plenty of wine and bread in your satchel." Just because she had conjured said fare meant nothing. She was unable to tell Erik not to eat from the old crone's table. For they were far from alone.

Abby turned away from him to dismount. The pain

made her bite into her cheek to avoid crying out. After all, what page would not have his seat in the saddle? *Foolish. How could I not have thought about this part of the journey? Maybe because I was too busy thinking about how to save Erik's retched hide.* She wasn't truly mad at Erik. She was mad at herself for not thinking about riding more beforehand. Abby had even spent time with her aunt, whom everyone told her to stay away from, in order to prepare for this inevitability.

"Sire, your reins." Abby waited patiently as her brother stared at her. She knew he was trying to figure out what she was up to, but he never would. Not this adventure. Another perhaps. Gran had stated there would be others, but these were her dreams. Her nightmares. Her demons to slay. After exchanging glares for reins, she made her way down the path toward the river.

Oh, how she relished the freedom of these britches. Out of sight of her brother and the crone, Abby startled the horses with a leap into the air. Something un-Thomas-like, but something she would do every day when no one was around. Joy burst forth, as sunshine on a spring morning after a hard winter. "Bloody hell," she practically dropped to her knees having forgotten how saddle sore her thighs were. Her lungs filled with the scent of pine, heated walnut and hickory to ease the pain. The crone did not visit this part of the wood.

Thankfully, it had never felt her taint. Curious squirrels, chipmunks and all types of birds began to chirp and twitter. They knew what she was and her greatest affinity. As much as she wanted to linger in the welcoming wood, she dared not. Her brother was alone with the hag and knowing the brain he most thought with, would succumb to her temptations.

Moving forward quickly, Abby found the edge of the river soon after her respite. The horses happily drank their fill as she sank her hands into the dark wet earth recharging herself with her element. Eyes closed, she exhaled completely and let her glamour fall. When a gasp, from behind her glamour snapped back into place with fire at her fingertips ready for battle. *How stupid to be caught in the open.*

"Begging your pardon, mi' lady." The servant bobbed slightly staring wide-eyed in Abby's direction.

"I'm no lady," she stated. "You will do best to forget all you've seen here and call me Thomas. Is that understood?" Abigail was prepared to bewitch the girl if she needed to, but thankfully the servant nodded quickly. Young she may be, but she understood how to survive in this world.

"Are ye here to kill the hag?" the young woman whispered.

"Why would you ask such a thing?"

"For she is evil and even I can see your light."

"No one has such light as you speak. Everyone has darkness inside of them."

"Aye. Yet one can embrace the light or the dark," the girl stated. "The old witch chose the darkness. She sacrificed her soul to it. I do not know why, but she will kill you both if you stay. Do not eat anything she prepares. I was sent to get water for her before I leave for the night."

"Why do you work for the crone if you do not like what she does?" she asked.

"Not all of us can be of noble houses, milady. Nor can we all have magic at our fingertips, but you--I sense you are more powerful than the old one and can end her devastation in these woods."

Abby, as Thomas, reflected upon the girl's words as she led the horses back to the crone's cottage. Surely. Erik would be smart enough not to eat or drink anything offered to him by the old witch. He couldn't be that blind to the glamor spell. *I swear if he lays with that old woman, I will never let him live it down. I shall put the image of a shriveled up old crone in his head every time he sees a beautiful woman, or male for that matter.*

The mumblings continued in her head until she was all but running, the horses trotting beside her back to the broken-down cottage. Yet Abby knew what other travelers would see; a beautiful cottage with a perfect thatch roof, lovely flowers, masonry without chips and yet she could see nothing but decay.

"Milord," she declared, rushing inside of the cottage, thankful to see her brother unharmed. "The horses are watered and ready for the next part of our journey."

"Thank you, Thomas, but we will be resting here for tonight. Our hostess has kindly given us lodging for the evening. With this late hour, it is unlikely we will reach our destination before dark."

"But, milord."

Erik raised a brow.

"What of the horses?" she scrambled for a response.

"My servant will show you where to put your tack and tether your horses for the night." The older witch smiled at the young girl.

"Thomas, return straight away as soon as the horses are taken care of. I'd like to turn in. I am rather tired and would like to start early in the morning."

"Aye, milord." Though she hated playing his servant, Abby understood the meaning behind Erik's words. Perhaps her brother wasn't such a wanker after all.

Erik rose the next morning with a crick in his neck, that's what he got for sleeping in a strange bed instead of his own. He'd known from the start Shona wasn't what she appeared to be. He'd felt the underlying evil under the sugary sweet exterior. 'Tis why he'd used his own form of magic to put her into a sweet slumber. He would let his sister think the worst, just to vex the brat, since she'd taken to insert herself into his business. Time to wake up the bratty princess. The early hour would put a feather in his brotherly revenge cap. The thought made him smile and the rough night worth the stiffness in his muscles.

Gloominess hung around the edges of the cottage. It oozed as puss from the very pores of nature. Erik saw the horses tethered on the outskirts of the yard; Abby rolled up in a blanket on the ground nearby. Sure, long strides carried him across the yard.

The toe of his leather boot met her covered backside. "Shake a leg, Thomas." Red curly hair hid the look she was giving him. "Daylight is burning, boy. Get the horses fed, watered and ready to go." Erik chose to ignore the choice words she called him as in the old days. Except this time. she couldn't go tattle to their parents on how "cruel" he was being towards her. In fact, the little minx was going to owe him when this was over. No amount of magic would get her out of the hot water she was in with their parents.

Erik needed to make use of the outhouse and headed in its direction. The crunch of dried leaves made him turn his head to see Abby making her way towards the horses. He had to give her credit. She had gotten right up and to work. Something he had doubted the spoiled princess would do, but he could see she had grown a lot in the last year. It made him wonder how much Mum and Gran had taught her, probably the basics along with the feminine potions. Useless magic. A rock hit him square between the shoulder blades making him frown and turn around to find Abby's glamour firmly in place. She was tending to the horses as if nothing had happened. Her time would come. Eventually. Right now, he would take care of getting the army from Lord Wellsley and enjoy watching his sister receive her comeuppance from their parents.

"You know she is not going to want us to leave without a proper breaking of the fast," his sister piped up at his return from his morning salutations.

Of course, he had to inspect her work. How ridiculous it would look if he fell off Holok because his saddle was not properly tightened. A quick glance at the horses, he gave her a little credit; she might actually know what she was doing for a change. But this was something Erik would not share with her. She had both groomed and one saddled. He had to admire the quick, sure strokes she gave his mount before helping her lift the heavy saddle on Holok's back.

"I know, Thomas, but we must not dawdle. We have bread and wine to fill your endless pit of a belly." He laughed then pat his sister's back. "I recall what it is like being a growing boy."

If daggers could fly out of the glare he received from that comment, well, he wouldn't have to worry about the hag. Loud laughter erupted making his steed sidestep and snort in startlement. "If you could see your face right now. Thomas, ah now, I mean no harm. I am sure the ladies like you right off. Especially the feeble minded such as my sister." It didn't surprise him when she made a feeble attempt to hit him on the nearest shoulder.

"Milord, Thomas," the servant girl cleared her

throat and bowed her head. Nervous but pretty. Not his type. He liked women with a touch of spirit, not virgins afraid of their own shadows. Then again, she was but a child. "My lady requests you break your fast with her this morning. She has been wo-o-orking hard to prepare a fine meal."

He finished saddling Holok ignoring the girl for the most part. "Tell your mistress we are unable to comply. We thank her for her hospitality, but it is imperative that we be on our way."

"Oh, but milord, please if you don't break fast, she'll be ever so furious."

Erik stood firm and shook head. The woman must have seen his head shake no from the cottage because when he looked up, he saw her walking fast across the yard with two cups in hand. Holding in a sigh, Erik put on a false smile. If only they had gotten out of there before the woman had woken up. Luckily when he had put her to sleep, he made her dreams happy, making her think she had gotten her way by bedding him.

"Milord if you won't stay for a meal perhaps this warm mead will fill your belly," the old witch held up the two cups. He finished saddling his horse, mounted, and turned to his sister.

"Thomas will bring the mead along. Thank you for your hospitality, sweet lady, but we must continue on our journey. Your kindness knows no bounds. I shall refresh myself on your delicious mead in less than a league," he stated.

Erik rode off leaving Abby to deal with the old hag. Let the womenfolk sort this out. He wouldn't travel far though. He was sure his sister was taught diplomacy by their mother and would be able to diffuse the situation immediately. If not, he would be close at hand to get her out of any magical traps she found herself caught in.

Of course, Erik would do something stupid like leave her standing here with an innocent and an evil witch. Well, at least he was currently safe, she hoped. Thieves roamed these woods rampantly and could be anywhere. *Brothers*. She exhaled heavily.

"Milady, please forgive milord," Abigail pleaded.

"He is anxious to get to our destination." As Thomas, she mounted Mondis and took one of the cups of mead. The smell, an enticing mix begging to be drunk.

"Be sure to give it to your master."

"Aye, milady. I shall indeed." The poor servant girl had tears in her eyes. Abby wished she could assure her she had no intention of allowing her brother to drink this potion of poison, but it would alert the old one of her plans.

Instead, she rode off a few paces, pulled out acorns and her athame from her satchel. It would take blood magic to counter the vital fluid the necromancer used to cast her depraved spells. Mondis stood perfectly still. He knew what she was about to do was imperative to the success of their mission. She balanced the mead between her thighs, pulled off her gloves and cut the palm of her hand. The blood dripped onto the acorns as she whispered words of transformation. She squeezed her hand revealing a necklace. One, once placed around the crone's neck would take her life.

"Perfect, Mondis. Even if I should say so myself." Taking hold of the mead, Abby turned the horse back toward the cottage in all haste. Afraid she would spill it on Mondis, she tossed it into the animal's pen.

"Milady," as Thomas, she shouted, approaching the cottage. "I almost forgot. Milord has a gift for you."

She saw a wave of the old woman's hand, but since Abby had always seen the cottage for what it was, the glamour was lost on her. It made her smile; a reminder to pretend that all was beautiful and bright.

"A gift for me?"

"Aye, milady." The acorns were presented as rubies and diamonds. "They were to be a gift for the Lady Wellsley, but milord said they reminded him much more of your passion." The woman grabbed greedily at the necklace. Abby bowed to hide her smirk and backed away from the nag before trotting off.

However, she came to a halt and dismounted at the animal pen. Where she had tossed the mead now lay a dead goat. "Bloody hell, Mondis. Goddess's Grace that could have been you." She kissed the horse on the nose before approaching the make-shift fence. "I did not mean to hurt you, Gilly," she said to the dead animal. A raven's cry called back to her. "Get away from Gilly or you shall become our dinner." A caw and nothing as she watched the bird die before her eyes. *The necromancer's poison.* Careful not to touch either animal with her skin, she bagged the raven and put it in her satchel. The why of it now, she couldn't reason. She certainly wouldn't eat it or allow Erik to eat it, but she felt it would be needed.

"Come. Mondis, let us leave this wretched place."

Mounting the horse, her seat becoming more tolerant to the movement, she kicked Mondis into a canter to catch up to her brother. What she had done to their hostess and what she no doubt would do before this adventure was finished, would be shared with no one. It would be just another secret buried deep within herself like so many others. Many she wished she could share with Erik. Perhaps one day, when he married and accepted who he was always meant to be, but it would be far into the future. Gran had foreseen it.

THREE

THE INN

ABBY THOUGHT TOO hard about how she deliberately killed the hag. Guilt began to set in. All her life she had been taught to harm none if she could help it. The reasoning behind this death be damned, even if she did save Erik's life. The servant girl was now free from evil and the abuse which she endured for a few pence. It was the first time Abby had taken a life. In all her teachings she'd only been taught what to do, she wasn't sure if she should feel grateful for her gran, and mother's lessons. Mentally shaking off the negative thoughts, she sucked in a lungful of air and looked at her brother's back. When the time came and she answered for her sins on the earthly plane, there would be solid reasons for her actions. May the Goddess grant her absolution for her choices.

The day dragged on and on as they made their way to the destination. Lost in her thoughts, Abby didn't think Erik would ever stop so she could at least get feeling back in her numb arse. He must have felt her eyes on his back because he turned in his saddle and gave her a look.

"You're awfully quiet today, sis, should I gander traveling like a peasant doesn't suit you?" Ignoring his jab, she plastered a fake smile on her face.

"By no means do I enjoy not having any feeling left in my legs, and arse while my belly eats away at my backbone."

"Since Thomas should have packed the saddlebags before you dragged him off to the nearest haystack. There might be some dried meat in my…" Before he could finish, she urged her horse closer to her brother's in order to plunge her hand into Erik's leather bag. Victorious, she pulled out the satchel of food. Thank the Goddess for small miracles. "Hey now, don't be greedy." Abby moved before her brother could snatch it out of her hand, opening the material her hand disappeared inside the bag.

"What? The all-sustaining male is hungry?" Biting into the hard dried meat, her taste buds hated the flavor, but her belly rejoiced.

"Not as much as you seem to be, brat." A piece of

meat flew towards his head, Erik managed to catch it with one hand.

"Tell me how much longer are we going to be before we call it a day?" Abby asked after finally eating enough to keep her stomach from complaining.

"Not too long." Was all he said, the damn stubborn man would have left it at that, thinking it was sufficient enough. Abby rolled her eyes mentally.

"Not too long, meaning? We ride until hell freezes over or the sun sets for the day?" she inquired as sweetly as she could manage.

"The sun won't set for a while yet." A heartbeat passed, and Abby gritted her teeth expecting more of an explanation, but no her dumb arse brother just gave her a smug grin and picked up the pace of his horse forcing her to do likewise.

"Why must you be so stubborn? I swear by the Goddess, Erik I am going to zap your horse's hindquarters just to watch you fall off," she yelled at his disappearing backside. The know-it-all sound of his laughter trailing behind him, only indication he'd heard her threat. Goddess save her from this irritating, pig-headed, dim-witted male her mother birthed and her future king. It made her wonder why she tagged along to save him in the first place.

"I love you too, Abigail," he laughingly taunted from a ways ahead.

"Mondis, why do I put up with his shenanigans?" she asked her horse. The steed did not answer but seemed to trot faster to keep up with the fading beat of Holok's hoofbeats pounding against the earth. Soon they were at a gallop. Trees flew by to give way to more frequent cottages, bridges, and a wider path. Soon, she caught up to her brother after lagging behind him for what had seemed like forever.

"What is this place?" she asked.

"Where we are staying the night," he answered.

"You couldn't have told me this before?" The frustration evident in her tone.

"Why ruin the fun of making you drop your glamour?" Abby gasped and pulled up her magic to make her appear to be Thomas again. In the nick of time, they entered a small village. Sheep bleated, as dirty children chased each other in reckless abandon, while they slowly made their way through its muddy pathways. Young and old alike would stop and gape at them being the strangers they were. Keeping her face from showing any emotions she made sure to stick close to Erik like the dutiful servant. *It would be nice to stop for the day,* she thought. *A nice hot non poisoned meal. Someone other than Erik to converse with or look at.* The pleasant thoughts almost caused her to grin from ear to ear, when they came to a stop in front of an Inn. Loud rambunctious noise could be heard through the wooden walls. This time, when Abby got off Mondis she was more careful, and made sure to regain the feeling in her legs before moving to follow Erik inside.

Erik's eyes took in the room at large, scoping out a place he could sit with his back against the wall. The smell of ale and unwashed bodies mingled in the air. Rough looking highwaymen sat in a group on the left-hand side of the room near the cooking fire. Dark eyes taking in everyone and everything happening in the Inn. They were trying a little too hard in his opinion to blend into the background. A drunk was slumped over his tankard, a trail of spittle rolling down the corner of his mouth from too much ale and not enough food. He looked over his shoulder to see Abby's glamour was firmly in place as her eyes widened while taking in the normal chaos a place like this always contained. He hid his laughter well at the disdain she held for the men in the room. She may look like his squire, but she didn't act like him. Long deliberate strides took him across the room to the table next to the fireplace. A shuffling of feet let him know Abby was close on his heels. The air wasn't as pungent, and the smell of baking bread made his belly growl.

"Sit." Erik commanded while seating himself with the wall protecting his back. The waitress appeared at his side making sure to show plenty of cleavage as she bent over the table to give it a quick swipe.

"What'll it be today, guvnor?"

"A couple pints of your ale and a room for the night if you've one free." Erik winked at the barmaid, pouring on a little bit of the charm.

"Ale and a room be yours, but if you've meat to share in exchange, it'll be your payment. These woods are not kind to us as of late." The buxom barmaid leaned closer giving him the full display of her ample chest. He chose to ignore the snort desertion coming from Abby. Flicking off a stray piece of food from the table, he smirked at his sister.

"Thomas, if you plan on making it in this world,

always remember to treat the ladies no matter age or looks, like they're the best thing you've ever seen," he took the maid's hand and kissed the back of it. "I believe my Page can arrange meat for a delicious stew to go with that wonderful smelling bread." He tried not to laugh when Abby bit her lip to keep a smart retort from leaving her mouth.

"Of course, only Inn patron's will be at dinner and we will be forever thankful," she gushed. Erik then received a breath stealing hug when she pulled his face into her mountain of flesh.

"I know you're still green behind the ears," he stated to Abby, "but I'll show you what you've been missing out on when we reach our destination."

"I don't need you to show me anything," she hissed.

"Of course, you do, first time outside of your mama's bosom."

"Just shut up, Erik. Thanks to you I have to go retrieve our precious dried meat from our satchels." He covered his mouth to hide his merriment at her red-haired temper. It seemed he always knew how to push the right buttons to irritate her the most.

He did watch her leave, only to make sure the ruffians remained seated. It only took a look of warning on his part to pull it off. The front door swung open and closed as people came and went. Abby returned, holding the ruck sack close to her chest. She plopped down on the bench heavily as Erik sipped from the pint the waitress had brought. Two empty bowls had been set on the table between them.

"Do not eat when the stew is served," Abigail warned in a hushed tone.

"What did you do, and why did you do it?" Erik asked.

"Get some bread and we can turn in early. Then I will tell you."

Erik tossed some coins down on the table. "Get the food and more ale then, I'll meet you in our room. It's the closest to the backstairs." Abigail scooped up the coins, gave him a quick nod and headed to the bar. He downed his pint, stretched and when he knew Abby was safe, went up the backstairs, knife palmed for the brigand who rose to follow him.

At the top of the stairs, he rounded the corner and waited for the male who was following him. Surprise and timing were everything, waiting for the moment the man rounded the corner Erik balled up his fist waiting to strike. Coiled up as a viper, he was determined to remind Abby he was a warrior and did not need a slip of a girl to protect him. As the thug came around the corner, Erik swung with such force, he heard the satisfying sound of bone breaking and cartilage tearing. It released some inner demon Erik did not know had possessed him. Before the male could call out to his friends, he followed the punch with a strangle hold. Erik kept his arm tightly around the highwayman's throat until it knocked him out cold.

The nearest watering closet turned out to be the perfect place to stash the heavy limp body just in time to find out what his sister was up to before they turned in for the night.

After a good night's rest, Erik made his way downstairs to Abby's room. A hard knock had her grousing at his intrusion, but he didn't care. A quick drawing of sigils to unlock her door and he had slipped inside. Erik grinned at her sleep-tousled hair. "Hey, princess, why did I go to bed hungry?"

"Because you are a fool not to have eaten the bread and jerky from your satchel?" Abby yawned, stretched and tossed the feathered pillow at his head. "Why are you here waking me so early? Are we leaving now?"

"Soon, but I want to know why I could not eat the stew. It smelled divine," he stated. Erik planted his feet firmly on the floor to rest his forearms on his knees. His sister's heavy sigh was the only indication she was going to answer him.

"I put magically enhanced meat in the stew to

bewitch patrons into a deep slumber for the night. Now can I go back to sleep? They will not wake for hours."

"You what? Abigail, you cannot just turn a roadside Inn into your own personal--"

"I put a spell about the Inn warning travelers away. Besides, those fools you sought company with were highwaymen and planned to kill you and rob you blind." Abby climbed from the bed and began to dress.

Erik gave deep thought to this adventure his sister had taken. He had to give it to her, she was taking this "watching his back" a little too seriously. Little girls and their magic should be at home around the hearth. *A discussion with Father is definitely needed to find a suitor that can tame her wild ways and keep her in check.* He amended his thought as they descended the stairs to include tame, but not break her wild ways. He couldn't imagine Abigail any other way than how she behaved now.

"Abigail," his voice barely above a whisper. Erik stood in the entrance to the main room of the Inn. It was as quiet as a grave. For good reason. Twelve people lay dead, scattered throughout the room.

"What?" Abby bit out. "Oh, dear Gods," her trembling voice replied.

"I don't think the Gods had anything to do with this, Abby. Get your horse saddle and your arse upon it. We will talk more as we ride. I think you have more to confess, do you not?"

Her silence told him more than her words could; then too, so did the fear upon her face. Good, he thought. Let her be afraid. Mayhap it will teach her not to try to be a man. The fact she had it struck in her craw; she was protecting him made him frustrated. The problem being she didn't think he could protect himself; as if he were so green behind the ears, he needed a woman to keep his hide intact.

Erik mumbled under his breath about his sister butting her nose in where it didn't belong. He used his magic to hide their presence making sure no one would be the wiser when they came into the empty establishment that the Prince and Princess of Mórrígan had spent the night. Angry strides ate up the ground when he got outside. Abby was already on her horse holding Holok in place as he danced around, no doubt feeling his emotions. Two seconds he was mounted and galloping out of town with his sister hot on his heels. Once they were only a half hour away from the village, he finally slowed down to a walk.

"Never do that again. What you thought as harmless caused inexcusable death." Erik held up his hand when Abby opened her mouth to speak. "Don't give me the malarky of saving my arse. You need to get it out of your curly red head. I don't need you, of all people, to keep me safe. I hate to be the bearer of bad news, but I *know* how to do that without your help. Been around a lot longer than your young arse has. How dare you warp Mother's and Gram's teachings. Killing someone for a selfish act is unacceptable. I hope the peaceful night's sleep was worth it."

What did I do wrong? No one should have died. I didn't put a single harmful root in the stew. Abby went over the previous afternoon repeatedly in her mind. The only thing she did was hand the cook the raven and seasoned the boiling water with her concoction of herbs. She was positive of it. Having Erik remind her of the Witch's Creed made her skin hot as if she were ready to explode. How dare he presume--

"Don't you ever speak to me in this manner again,

Erik, kiss my arse, I'm the bloody Prince who is perfect in all things, Lugh. I did not intend to kill anyone, ever. I sprinkled innocuous herbs into the boiling water, and I gave the raven to the...," she drifted off a moment. "I gave the raven," she whispered.

The raven. It had to be it. She had taken the raven from the old witch who was going to poison them. The mead the necromancer had made from it had killed a goat in an instance. She had no doubt the sorceress would have killed them both in the time it had taken for them to breathe and stored their hearts for her own use.

"Stop making up your crazy stories and face the facts, Abigail. Women should be at home with a man who can control their behavior."

"You have no idea where women belong, Your Highness, nor do you have any idea what our own mother has done to help our father in the name of being a woman. You are the one who is short-sighted, Erik. I pray the Goddess allows me to be there when you finally find happiness, for it will take probably more than one strong heart to meet your ideal of perfection." Abby was so angry. She pulled back on her reins causing her horse to rear and charge forward. Dumb arse of a brother. To yell at her and accuse her of breaking their most sacred of laws. Who did he think he was? Furthermore, who did he think she was? She was not like their mother's sister. To Abby, all life was precious.

"Big talk from one so inexperienced at knowing what they are capable of."

"As if you know the strength of your powers. You do not as Gran has stated time and again. You are the one who avoided their lessons." Finished with her pig-headed brother, she urged her horse to begin walking once more. "You are just like our brothers, Goddess keep them, thinking your male strength will get you through any fight. It did not help them now did it?" A tear had the audacity to roll down her ruddy cheek.

"You have it all figured out. Bravo sis. I bow before your Goddess knows how I, such a lowly male who needs a sprite of a female to protect my arse against all foes." Erik sarcasm rolled off his tongue while bending at the waist in a mock bow.

"Blimey, but this is a first. I thought you only bowed down to pay homage between a woman's thighs, or are you bullheaded enough to make her ride your face always? No matter. *Our* Goddess is aware that a lowly male, like the Prince, beloved by his sister and in need of a protector, should be sent a sprite to keep him safe." With a smug curve to her lips, Abby kicked her horse to go a touch faster leaving her red hair blowing in the wind.

"Bravo, Abigail." He hollered at her backside. "It would have been more meaningful if your stubborn arse wasn't going the wrong way." When her head whipped around, she saw he'd turned his mount deeper into the woods off the main trail. "Besides," he continued when she caught back up with him, her cheeks only a little flushed. "Not a single woman I've bedded ever complained about their glorious night with me."

Abigail gave an all over body shudder at the imagery his words placed in her mind. Just what she needed. The mental picture of her brother and some hapless woman naked entwined together, a sipid smile upon the maid's face.

"You do know how to ruin a morning," she groused.

"I'm not the one who killed an Inn full of customers," he snarked.

Her eyes narrowed; lips thinned. A small part of her wished she had stayed home and let him die alone at the crone's cottage.

"I should have let you die," she mumbled to herself. "Don't talk to me if I am that horrible. I may lose track of who I am saving and kill you off myself." With his back to her, she stuck her tongue out at him.

FOUR

THE CASTLE

THE RIDE FELT LONGER than it had the day before. Instead of taking the main road, Erik had them blindly riding into the woods dodging low lying branches. Abby knew he was doing it on purpose just to torture her over the incident at the Inn. She felt bad it'd happened; it hadn't been her intention to hurt anyone. She was just making sure they would be safe, but this is what happened when blood magic was used. It was unpredictable and the price was enormous. Gran had pounded it into her and her cousin, Agnes' heads many times. This type of divination should only be used when absolutely necessary. As a last resort.

With Erik being his egotistical arse self, the trip to Wellsley Manor felt if it took weeks, not mere hours. One thing was clear to Abby though, if another branch snagged her hair, she would knock the bloody bastard off of his holier than thou steed. Spires rose shouting their glory to the Gods of the Air. She snorted at the pretentiousness. Even their castle was not boastful enough to shout at the elements. Their castle welcomed the elements and became part of its surroundings. The only way anyone could penetrate the castle proper would be by treachery.

"I cannot believe Father wants Lord Wellsley's help." Abby finally broke the silence between the two.

"Oh, you are finally speaking to me again? Besides, how would you know things of war and planning battles? Father does not include you in his planning."

"No, he does not, nor does he include you. Which is why you are such a bloody piss ant these days. Stop taking it out on me because he sent you on this errand rather than ask your opinion of battle strategies," she shot back at her brother. *I see things haven't changed.*

"Fix your glamour, you spoiled brat. You know nothing about what it takes to win a war and if you try to say neither do I, I will knock you on your arse, sister or not."

"If you would look, milord, I am not your sister, but your friendly Page." She squeezed her thighs, urging her horse into a trot. It was her responsibility to announce Erik's arrival as they approached the castle guards.

After all the fan fair of meets and greets with everyone, Erik was able to finally have a formal meeting with the king. Even though his sister stood in the background ready to fetch at his beck and command, he was unsure if she'd behave and not speak out of turn.

"Prince Erik, although it is good to see you, I'd rather have your father here to discuss the business at hand."

"I understand, sire, but due to unforeseen circumstances he was needed elsewhere. You understand as you are in the same position of power. Have no fear, I am just as worthy as my father, or he wouldn't have entrusted me to talk with you about your agreement."

"Yes well, that has yet to be determined."

Erik started spouting off all the information he'd learned from his father, about Wellsley's troops. How many there were in attendance, and their prowess on the battlefield. He used his vast knowledge to convince the man how, by aligning himself with Mórrígan, would not only benefit Wellsley, but strengthen their solidarity as a kingdom. The more he talked, the more Wellsley became impressed, and deeper into his cups. "Darn me if your father hasn't done a fine job of raising you right." Wellsley slurred pounding his cup on the table to summon a servant to fill his goblet. Instead, his willowy blonde daughter came, casting side eye glances Erik's way.

"I see you are giving away the keys to the kingdom again, Father," the Princess stated.

"Ah, Ciara, my beautiful daughter. You are always keeping your father straight. What a wonderful consort you will make." Wellsley stated pride in his slurred speech.

Wellsley was inebriated enough that he didn't see the disdain in his daughter's eye at his words. This one would be Queen, Erik thought. He dared to look over his shoulder to find his own sister waiting impatiently for something to do. A bored Abby was never a good thing.

"Tell me, Prince Erik, do you have a wife, or may

we solidify our agreement with a true joining of kingdoms?"

The Princess gasped, Erik choked on his wine and his blasted sister burst out laughing. It startled him and others in the room as it sounded like an ill dog. Something high and low pitch at the same time when she remembered who she pretended to be.

"No," he practically shouted. "No, Sire. I have no wife." He wiped his mouth with the back of his hand, suddenly nervous as to why his father sent him on this mission. "The Princess is beautiful," he stood to his full height towering over Wellsley's firstborn.

"Ciara, mind your manners. Welcome Prince Erik to our home," the King chastised.

"I believe you have already welcomed him enough for the both of us, Father," Ciara stated.

Erik walked slowly around the girl as if inspecting fresh goods. He gave the girl credit, her back straightened as he rounded her backside, breath quickened as he got closer. Wife material. Well, he wasn't looking for a wife. Not one who didn't know her place in this world. This Princess needed a strong hand. Erik had that in spades, but he was looking more for a good time between the sheets though.

"The Princess is beautiful, strong, and would probably bear several children, but I am afraid I am not looking for a wife at this time. When I am ready to settle down..."

"When *you* are ready to settle down?" Ciara spoke up. Venom dripping with each syllable. "What if I don't want to marry you? Who says you are any prize as a husband?"

"Sit down, child." Wellsley urged Ciara. "Boy, you may be a Prince, but when a King offers his daughter in marriage, you accept. My agreement with your father is null and void."

"Sire," Abigail spoke up from her position in the back of the room. "If I may," she bowed low then quickly moved to Erik's side. "Milord has had a harrowing trip and needs to rest to consider the ramifications of your offer." He pinched his sister to get her attention. All he got was his foot stomped.

"Tell your Lord, he should think before he speaks," Lord Wellsley stated.

"Do you like riddles, sire?"

Will she ever shut up?

"Oh, look Father, the little boy likes to play games."

Please don't, Abby. Don't make this worse.

"Yes, young Page, I do."

Fuck me. He was going to strangle his sister. How he would explain her death to his parents, he didn't know. Maybe he by marrying the blonde Princess, keeping her knocked up and telling his mother she was Abby's replacement.

"If you cannot answer my riddle, you will honor your agreement with the Kingdom of Mórrígan and Prince Erik leaves with your army. If you guess the answer to my riddle, the Prince must return to King Mórrígan and tell him of his failure. Do you agree?"

"You are an insolent servant," Princess Ciara had no clue she was calling the kettle black.

"Aye," Erik stated. "You have no idea just how insolent. Whipping, or a sound beating does not help. He is loyal as they come to our kingdom. Will you play his game, or shall we leave, and I spread the word how you do not honor your agreements because of a vain woman?"

He received a shut the fuck up look from his sister. It made him smirk. Maybe she was trying to help him. If he didn't have to marry the Princess, he might forgive her for following him.

Whispered words between the King and Princess reached his ears. Every now and again he heard a word or two. Nothing which gave away their plan, unfortunately.

Concentrating on the royals gave him the excuse not to meet Thomas', aka, Abigail's mean gaze. What could she do to help this situation truly? Some foolish woman's riddle?

"We accept your terms. Prince Erik, you would do well to listen to your servant."

He snorted but bowed for Abby to approach the King and Princess.

"So that my Lord may rest for the night, you have until the break of fast in three days' time to give me your answer. Here is my riddle, one killed none, but still killed twelve."

"One killed none, but still killed twelve," Princess Ciara repeated.

"Aye," Erik stated. "Now, if it pleases you, sire, I shall retire for the evening." He bowed low pondering the riddle himself. While the Princess and her father began tearing apart the puzzle. A squire showed him and Abby to their quarters. After the heavy wooden door closed Erik turned on his heel to nail his sister with a glare which stopped her in her tracks. "What the hell are you trying to do to me?"

"I'm trying to save your mission, you foolish arse. That Princess doesn't want to marry you any more than you want to marry her. You jeopardize our armies for your pride, and you ask me what I'm doing? Good Goddess, Erik. You could agree to a handfasting for one year. You don't have to marry her till death do you part, as Mother and Father have done." Red curls and familiar features returned as she berated him. It struck him as funny to see her dressed as Thomas with wild curls everywhere.

"Go to your room. Stay out of trouble. For once," he added with a chuckle.

"I should say the same to you, *Milord*. Pray to the Goddess they do not guess the answer and we can be on our way home. I miss Mother's nightly hair brushing and talks of wisdom."

It didn't surprise him at all that their mother did such things. He vaguely remembered her doing the same for him. Now, when he was home, he spent his time with his father. Hearing his sister speak of time with their mum, made him a bit jealous of having her attention. Mayhap when they returned, he would request lunch with her to discuss his sister's wild ways. Erik sighed, after his sister left. He just needed to get through this mess she'd created then everything would work itself out. He had to believe it, or he'd snatch every red hair out of Abby's head for putting him in this predicament. A timid knock on his door brought him back from his internal thoughts. *Now what?*

"Enter."

"Sire," A wisp of a maid pushed open his door. "The Princess told me to see if there was anything you needed?" The minx slid into his room and closed the door behind her. "I'm ever eager to please your every desire." Erik's eyes took in her low-cut dress, and cap sleeve which fell off her shoulder to expose a plump breast to his gaze. He wondered what the Princess promised her for coming to his room and offering up her services.

"I have a need for many things." He replied sitting down in the chair, deciding to let the game play out. Why not there was nothing else to do, cocking his head indicating his boots she sashayed over to straddle one leg, then his other once she took off each leather shoe. Making a bold move she straddled his lap and rubbed her hands up and down his chest, before unlacing his pants to stroke the bare skin exposed underneath.

"Sire. What is this riddle you Squire spoke of? One killed none, but still killed twelve. The castle is all abuzz about this puzzle." Small strong hands squeezed his male member causing a hiss of arousal to leave his lips. So, this was the game afoot. Sexual favors for the answer to the riddle.

"It's naught anything to worry your pretty little head about." He told her before standing up, her bum cupped in his hands to keep wrapped around his waist. "Besides, there are better things to talk about than castle gossip." Over the course of the night, he was visited by every young maid servant in the kingdom, or so it seemed. Either one, two, or three at a time, it became a blur of sexual need and fulfillment before the sun started raising its rays the next morning. Each one asked him about the riddle hoping to get the answer out of him. Since the riddle was Abby's, he had no answer for them, no matter what sexual acts they performed, he evaded and enjoyed each and every minute of the long night. However, come morning, he would pry the answer from his stubborn sister one way or another.

When Abigail left the room, heading to her own was not on her agenda. Not when she had waited, what seemed like forever, to come to Wellsley without the ever-watchful eye of her mother and visit Orla, an ancient witch known to dabble in dark magic. Every time she asked questions, her mother would shush her, or put off her query till when they were alone but would find a reason not to answer her at all. Now was her chance and she wasn't going to miss it.

Slipping out of the castle was easier than she expected. Nothing seemed to change in Wellsley. It would be simple to conquer should anyone choose to do so. Mayhap she should whisper this to Erik. After all, he would not allow the Princess to remain Queen for long if he had to marry her. The girl had eyes for more than Wellsley and if she were to look at Mórrígan, she would be wise to reconsider. Thankfully, she had no other brothers to fall prey to the vixen's beauty. It was well the magic in Wellsley was weak. But a worry for another day. Today was for learning a different type of magic.

"Merry meet, Orla," she called out. "Abigail Mórrígan here to learn the lessons you would teach."

The dilapidated door on the cottage creaked in protest. An illusion, she knew, but one necessary to keep out those who did not belong. It grew difficult for Abby to hold her powers at bay. She was excited to be here, and she made the dead trees bloom. Flower bulbs burst forth with life and she laughed plucking a rose.

"Get inside, child, before you turn this wood into a rainforest." Doing as she was told; she quickly entered the warm and welcoming home of the crone. "What brings you to my lair without your mother?" Orla placed tea in front of Abby.

"You knew I was coming?"

"Of course, child. The Goddess told me you were on an adventure. I bet your mother will be livid when you return home. Especially when she discovers you come to talk to me about blood magic. You've spied upon your aunt and you've used it in combat. Be wary, for it is of our darker selves. Only the Goddess can lead you using her blood." Orla took hold of her now healed hand.

"I have spied upon my aunt and I do not trust her. She is vicious. I fear for my cousin's life. Yet my mother will not discuss it. In my heart I know I need to help Agnes. I must. She is a part of me."

"Aye, more than you know," the crone murmured. "The Goddess could provide you with the answers."

"She led me to you."

Laughter filled the room. They sat in welcoming silence drinking their tea and taking each other's measure.

"If I were to teach you this magic, what would you do with it?"

"Help Agnes if I can. Help my people, most definitely. Help my parents, if they will allow it, but for sure harm none, for I have inadvertently harmed already."

The evening passed quickly. She was tired of practicing lifting herself in the air and holding herself at a steady height. Orla was happy with her progress though and said she would be able to harvest Dittany of Crete without dying. All a good thing, in her opinion. Being able to talk and summon the dead would be useful. She had already thought of ways it could help. As did wormwood, which she already had in her satchel.

They discussed additional uses of Monkshood, Aconite, Yew, Mandrake and Asphodel. "What about using lavender and apple?" Abby asked. "I know they are typically used to ward off evil, but I overheard my aunt--"

"Yes," Orla answered. "They can be used to communicate with the dead. As with almost everything, even these beautiful things can be used for evil if they are warped by magic. Magic is innocuous. Magic just is. How it is used determines whether it is good or harmful."

Orla told her the things she had been taught her whole life. Everything she said were things her gran and mother had taught her. So, if she had been told this by her grandmother and mother, then surely her aunt had learned it as well. It perplexed her to know that her

Aunt Caitriona knew this but did the opposite. Why would she?

"I know that bewildered gaze. Mayhap a taste of power, jealousy, vengeance, or plainly a black heart. Only the Goddess could say what caused Caitriona to choose her path. There may be machinations at work which we know nothing about."

For the first time since her reckoning day, Abigail thought about sitting with her gran and watching a book of moving pictures. "Mayhap," she whispered. "Gran showed me a book once and said Erik and I would be needed one day to help a fellow witch fight a great battle."

"I have no doubt the witch will be grateful. Come child, I've a place you can rest before you return to your brother."

"I am not even going to ask how you know I am with my brother."

"I could say that his prowess with the ladies had them twitterpating his arrival, but the truth is a little bird told me you headed this direction."

Orla laughed at her own joke and Abby couldn't help but join in. Abby lay on the cot long after Orla fell into slumber. She'd learned much in one evening. Would her mother be angry, or would the Queen be proud her daughter found the answers she needed and was learning how to protect her home? Temperament would be required, of course. Something Erik said she needed, badly. Only when it came to dealing with her stubborn arse brother. Thinking of him, alone, with the Princess and her attitude put a Cheshire grin on her face. It would serve her brother right to be saddled with a bossy, fiery, passionate woman for the rest of his life. May the Goddess make it so.

Sleep captured Abigail, but it was not the sleep of lovers embracing one another in the night. No, it was something else entirely. The wind howled. It was daytime, yet the sky darkened. She felt magic in the air and ran. Fear clogged her throat. Icy fingers gripped her heart; the why of it she could not say. Flashes of her mother's face, her father's smile. Blood and demon red eyes made her wake with a start. Sweat dripped down her face. She felt as if she had been truly running through her home searching for her parents. It must have been the tea. She wasn't used to such a strong mixture. Mayhap it unsettled her stomach. *Yes, that must be my ailment.* She thought hard about her dream, though specifics were already beginning to fade away, leaving only fragments of foreboding behind. She wished she could speak to Erik about it, but he would tell her it was a silly dream of a silly, spoiled brat of a girl.

Gran would know what to make of it. *So, do you. Just give yourself time to sort it out. You know exactly what the dream was telling you. Just think.*

Think she tried. But the tendrils of slumber pulled her back into its depths and with her premonition all but forgotten.

Erik stretched and looked over at the last maid who had come to visit him. He was a little tired and a lot hungry from the work out he'd gotten during the dark hours of the night. He decided to get up and find sustenance to survive the coming day. Dressed and out of the room on silent feet, he made his way to where Abby's room was. They needed to have a talk about this riddle. Two floors down he came upon the main room containing only a few people. A small, framed male darted the edge of the room heading towards the servant's quarters. Abby. What or who the hell had she been doing this early in the morning? Following closely, Erik scared her literally out of her skin when his hand landed on her shoulder to stop her in her tracks.

"Where do you think you're going? You have been scarce the last two days while I've had to endure the Princess and the King."

"Bloody hell, Erik. Are you trying to send me to an early grave?" she asked. "Though it looks like you may have been pulled from one. I am sorry you had to survive on your own volition. Have you gotten no sleep?"

"No thanks to your riddle. I had maids interrogating me every night to find out the damn answer."

"Interrogating you? More like you bedding them." Damn him, but to make her point one of the lovely playthings from early in the eve passed by offering a satisfied smile and to bring him anything he needed. "I see just how well you were interrogated," the brat smirked.

"That is beside the point." He told her after they were alone again. "Where were you?"

"I was visiting a friend," she said. The fact she flipped nonexistent hair off her shoulder gave the impression he would not approve of this friend.

"What friend? So, help me Abigail if you--"

"It was Orla. I spent the time with Orla learning from her. It's not as if you missed me."

"You know Mother would skin your hide if she knew you were around Orla without her knowing. You have no clue what that witch is capable of, and don't give me any of your lip about last night. It's your mouth that made it happen." He whispered the last since there was yet another maid coming towards them with a smile on her face. As she passed him her body rubbed against his knowingly.

"Good morning, sire. If there's anything you need..." She trailed off giving him a kiss on the cheek before whispering the rest in his ear.

"Oh bother, would you just leave off already." Abby snapped at the twittering maid. "Milord needs to have a moment to recover."

"It is not what he said last eve." She sniped back seeing Abby as Thomas, a young boy and insignificant. "Sire, just let me know if you have a need for me later." One last kiss and she left, but not before giving Thomas a glare. Erik had to keep from chuckling at the sight of his sister's face turning red.

"Don't drop your glamour over a slip of a girl, brat." He told Abby's backside, stomping to her room, only spinning around to flash him an obscene jester before going through the open doorway and slamming it closed. This time Erik did laugh out loud before leaving her to her own devices as he sought out something to eat. Goddess only knew what he was in for this coming day, and he would need all his strength to survive it.

A leisurely stroll around the yard proved futile. The clanging of metal against metal brought him to the area the sword practicing was being held. Groups were scattered around the yard exercising and being taught how to move the right way. Erik decided to join in, needing the distraction, and staying out of the sight of the many women he'd bedded last night would keep him from the game the Princess and her father were about. All because of Abby and her damn riddle to get Wellsley to give him their troops.

"Milord," Abby shouted over the clank of swords. "I've brought you something to fill your belly and ease your aching muscles." Was that a grin on Thomas's face, or did his sister truly mean to be of service to him? The sun was at just the right pitch he couldn't tell. "Come and sit, milord. Eat and I will lather you with this ointment, one of the maids left for you."

Definitely a grin. This was all her fault. Not that he didn't enjoy himself. He would eat the food and get some answers.

"Thank you, Thomas. Grab one of those short-bladed swords and you can help me in working out the kinks of last night. You know the places ointments won't work." Maybe the brat needed a lesson in humility. A good couple of hours of working muscles she didn't know she had would make her rethink about meddling in affairs of men.

He made her cry mercy only a half hour in. "Tsk, tsk, Thomas. If we're going to make you a man, you need to practice until you cannot practice anymore. Now pick up that sword and let's go again." Erik chuckled when his sister groused at him for abusing her in such a manner.

"You will pay for this brother," Thomas hissed.

"Aww, now. Thomas. If you want to be a knight one day, you must become strong," he gestured to all the men in the field. "We all learned what it took, didn't we men!" Erik shouted. The men shouted in return as he knew they would.

"You know how to move. I'll give you that. My other squire has taught you well. I shall remind him that swordplay is for men, until you prove otherwise." He wanted to laugh but getting his sister's red-haired dander up had him minding where she swung her sword.

"I would hate to disappoint the ladies, milord, by

accidentally cutting off part of your anatomy," Abby held the point of her sword near his groin. He was unsure if she would cut his balls off or not. Given the right frame of mind, he had no doubt she would.

"Mayhap it is time to bathe for this evening's meal," Erik offered with a bow. Erik could afford to give her this boon. She'd actually performed about as well as their mother. It would be loathsome to inform her of such details, so he would keep the information to himself. Besides, he wanted to learn the answer to the riddle and to do so, he would need Abigail to tell him the truth. Tit for tat.

"Aye, milord. It is almost time to address the King once more. He has until tomorrow to give us his answer."

"Speaking of the answer, tell me what it is," he asked her as they walked back toward the castle proper. "After all, you're the one who made up this ridiculous riddle."

"I am surprised you haven't guessed," her heavy breath raised the hair on his arm. "One killed none, is the poisoned mead which spilled upon a goat killing it. But still killed twelve--"

"A raven ate the goat, died and you fed the raven to the twelve who died at the Inn," he responded.

"Ah, but there is hope for you yet, brother. One day, when you are king, I will be happy to be your advisor."

What else could he do but laugh. "Women do not belong in a place of power. Women cannot handle power. It corrupts them."

"Says men who have small man bits and cannot think past the end of their nose." Abby retorted. "It isn't the power which corrupts. It is what one chooses to do with that power which determines your path. Mayhap Father should have kept you home to learn your Princely lessons. Prince Nolan will be a fine and just ruler one day. He appears eager to be like our father rather than his own. Is that your problem Erik? Do you follow another King's wisdom?"

"I will do what is needed in keeping our kingdom safe. If that involves following wisdom that I may not agree to, then so be it. Father has taught me to trust my instincts and how to handle politics from a young age. Whereas you have learned only what is expected of you and how to deal with it."

"So, say you. I believe my actions have proven otherwise. Since you do not live in the castle daily, you would not know what is expected of me, dear brother. Very little if I may be frank. I do many things to help which neither you, nor mother is aware of. Truthfully, I like it that way. No one needs to parade me about like a trophy. I am no man's decoration." Like a feral cat, she spat and hissed her displeasure. If he didn't know better, he would believe she was upset with him personally.

"I've never thought you'd be a simpering female bending down to any man. But you and I know one day you'll face your own reckoning just like you say I will. Now let's go eat so you can torment Wellsley about this riddle and I can finish what father sent me here to do."

The evening meal passed quietly due to the King eating in his chambers stating he had business to take care of and Princess Ciara made her excuses to check on her father. Erik thought he might have a peaceful evening once he dismissed his sister from his side.

"Thomas, please remain in the castle this evening," he stated. His servant huffed before nodding.

"Yes, milord. Shall I turn down your bed milord?" The sweet way in which it was asked told him to say otherwise, though it would have been nice.

"I can do that myself but thank you. I tossed and turned all night long," he said publicly. "Mayhap I will retire early to get the sleep I didn't receive last evening."

He should have known Abby would look at her pocket watch, gage how much time she had left and bowed quickly, quietly, excused herself, still with her

Thomas glamour, and headed up the stairs. Erik waited the appropriate time before heading to his room. The quiet of the room drew him in. Tonight, he'd rest up and get his final answer from Wellsley even if he had to visit the man in his room to do so. He'd removed everything but his pants when there was a knock on the door, wondering if Abby was going to bug him one last time before going to bed, he yanked open the wooden structure about to give her a piece of his mind. Only to find it was the Princess in a see-through nightgown. Every curve and valley prominent in the candlelight glowing behind her.

"I've heard about your prowess in the bedroom, sir. Since I am responsible for making sure guests are comfortable and happy with their stay, I thought I'd check to see if your every need was met last night." Like the maids she slipped into his room closing the only way out behind her. But she did it with grace and class. He had to give it to her, she was bound and determined to find out the answer of the stupid riddle just like the rest who came before her.

"I'm sure you also heard there weren't any complaints about my stay here nor your maids whom you sent to me last night." The Princess pulled the ties holding her flimsy material together so that it cascaded down her body to pool at her feet.

"You must show this stamina, sir. I have needs and none here fill them. But you, I know, can make my body sing in delicious ways it's never sung before. If I'm to go off what the maids have said about you." Never one to pass up an opportunity, he shook off his fatigue and showed the Princess how well he could make her body carry a tune. Stamina and Prince Erik would mean the same thing when he held up longer than any other man had before him. During the night, she tried to get the answer to the riddle. but he evaded. She knew sexual positions he'd never tried before. The Princess must have spent a lot of time at court to learn the moves she used on him. During one weak moment she prodded him again asking for the answer to the riddle. His mind was a little scrambled but not so far gone that he didn't know her game. Erik told her a half truth. He told her the riddle's end was a poison. His answer seemed to spur her desire even higher, and she rode him harder than she probably ever had with her steed, crying out for the whole castle to hear when she reached her pinnacle point of no return. Erik only held her in place when she tried to leave and proceeded to show her she wouldn't get her way and leave him wanting more.

The next morning, he woke up to the cold air brushing over his body when the Princess wrapped the sheet around herself and to leave his room. A well satisfied smile on her face as she left him naked and alone in his room. He was sure she was beaming inside over defeating him, at least she thought she had. Taking no time, he got dressed and packed his bag, tossing it at Abby when she came to his room only to wrinkle her nose at the smell of sex permeating the room. Ignoring her jabs at him for being a deprived male, Erik saw a flash of material lying on the floor that wasn't his, but Princess Ciara's. He picked it up and folded the barely there material and put it into his jerkin's pocket. A memento of his time of a night he enjoyed, even if there had been alternative motives.

"Get the horses ready while I grab us something to eat for our journey home," Erik said.

Abby nodded when she saw the look on his face. Determined steps carried him to the dining hall.

"Milord, do you have the answer I seek?" Erik asked when he was only a couple of feet from Wellsley.

"Of course, I do." The pompous man crowed giving his daughter he'd bedded a smug smile.

"Oh, please let me, Father." Getting the nod, she stood up, making everyone in the room stop talking to hear the answer. "It was a selective poison." Everyone cheered in the hall thinking the Princess had outsmarted him.

"*Wrong* answer." Abby stated, disguised as Thomas once again. The minx of course hadn't listened to him; she'd snuck up next to him to douse the flame of victory over the room.

"But he told me…" Realizing she would have to explain herself Princess Ciara sat down and looked anywhere but at her father.

"Yes, I did but not the right answer." A scream of outrage from her matched the one from her father, making Erik chuckle at the tantrum. "I will tell my father to expect your men in two days hence." Giving Wellsley a bow he spun on his booted heel and dragged Thomas with him. Forget the food. He suddenly felt an urgency to leave Wellsley and return home.

"Wait! You must tell us the answer." The King demanded. "Prince Erik, surely you will allow more time than two days?"

"You have already had three in which to prepare. By my reckoning, that is a total of five days to provision troops and your answer is a raven."

"It was a poisoned raven." Abby informed those gathered in the great room, only to be met with silence as they mulled it over, confused more so than before. "A crone filled with ill content tried to kill milord as we trekked through the forest. The raven became poisoned when I fed a goat the gruel which was met for Prince

Erik. In haste, I saved the raven only to have it be used in a stew at an Inn." Erik grabbed her by the upper arm and pushed her along no need to stick around any longer.

"Is this true, Your Highness?" the Princess sneered.

"You question a member of the Mórrígan family?"

"Family?" King Wellsley scoffed. "You consider your servants family?" Those in attendance began to laugh.

"Remove your glamour, Abigail. I am through with charades," he whispered. Truthfully, he planned on riding hard and all night if necessary until they reached home. Wellsley could try to get retribution for making him look like a fool in front of his people. The idiot deserved it. Erik knew his father would be pleased by doing what he'd set him out to do and that's what mattered the most he thought as they left behind the completed business, and headed home. It mattered naught to him the King was a fool. Mayhap the time had come for the Mórríganians to lay claim to this kingdom as well. No one questioned him, or his bratty sister. She did not lie to ensure his freedom. As a matter of fact, she would relish his predicament if he had been forced to wed the ambitious and power-hungry Princess.

"I am far from a servant, Milord," Abby retorted.

"You must forgive our charade, but it was imperative that I follow and protect my brother. The Goddess gave me such visions as she blesses my gran. Which is why you will send your men as promised. For I have been shown a great evil with red eyes and it is coming for us all. If Mórrígan falls, the Kingdom of Wellsley will be next."

"I am a man of my word, young Princess, or should I have your tongue for your insolence?"

Erik placed his free hand on the hilt of his sword and squeezed his sister's arm with the other. It would be a miracle if they were able to get to their horses without a fight.

"I mean no disrespect, sire. I only repeat what I saw as I trained with Orla, your seer and advisor."

To Abigail's credit, she bowed her head to Wellsley. There may be some hope for the brat after all. For now, though, they needed to leave, and he needed to learn more of this vision of hers.

"Your Grace, I shall tell my father to expect your regiment and how hospitable you were to one and all." He bowed his head and dragged his sputtering sister with him out the door. Horses awaited with a full night's ride ahead of them.

"Erik, we have to hurry," Abby kept up with him

stride for stride. "I have a bad feeling we are going to be cutting it close. Too close."

Mondis and Halleck were waiting for them as was Orla.

"The beast with red eyes has been summoned. You must ride like the wind, children, to reach them in time. I fear you will be too late."

He could not spare a moment for his sister's tender backside. Not when his father and mother needed him. He was already at a gallop before looking to see if Abby was following him. To his surprise, she was right behind him with the same determined countenance upon her face.

FIVE

MORRIGAN

AFTER TELLING Erik about her vision, they rode in silence for hours. Prayers to the Goddess whispered in Halleck's ear as she rode close to his neck for speed. The spell was but a simple one which would take her mind home, but the path for Halleck must remain straight and true.

"Erik," she called out. "Can we stop at the next rise?" It would anger him, she knew, but the horses needed the rest, even if it were for but a few moments, and she needed to give her mind peace.

"We need to keep going," he responded. "If we stop every time your arse gets sore—"

"Stop it. Just give me but a few minutes to check Mórrígan."

"Your little bit of sparkly magic isn't going to do shite to help the situation, Abigail."

His anger and worry were palpable, and she hated to admit that sparkly magic wouldn't help, but she knew a lot more than mere parlor tricks thanks to Orla's training.

"Your ring please," she held her hand out flat. "I'll return it right away. I promise." It was his ring marking him as the heir. She held it in her hand and opened her third eye to see their homeland. Erik could do the same if he didn't think it was weak female magic. It would be a handy tool to use when you wanted to spy. Unless, of course, wards were set up to protect against such things, but who would believe that the Prince or Princess of Mórrígan would spy upon the King and Queen let alone the people in the kingdom. Yet, Abby was about to do just that. Spy in order to assure the demon had not entered her home.

"What do you see?" Erik asked.

"Open your magical eye and see," she whispered. A ghost of a figure in the castle, she took hold of Erik's hand pulling him along for the magical ride.

"Where is everyone?" he asked.

"I fear we are too late, or could the castle be preparing to fight?"

"Let's damn well hope they are getting ready to fight. We've got to get home, Abby."

"Together we can make a portal Erik. I can direct it to open in the upper gardens." She was afraid he would say no. If he did, they still had half a day to ride before they would reach their destination. It was only adrenaline, fear and worry which kept them on their feet as it was.

"Fuck me, Abigail. How do you know these things? I never wanted you to learn such magic."

"My destiny is in shadows, Erik. You are there, but it is volatile, and I am afraid. I need Mother to be with me. Take my hand." At his firm grasp, her eyes began to glow as her magic rose to mix with his. They stretched forth their free hand together and magic poured forth. Soon, the fabric of space split as if a doorway opened. Rather than woodland, beautiful flowers and rushes filled the small area. It was just enough for them to lead their horses from the borders of Mórrígan to the gardens at court.

Otherworldly screams rent the air. Abby did not hide the fear in her gaze. She dropped her steed's reins and ran after Erik. His sword already unsheathed, he headed into the battle which commenced in the courtyard. She needed to find her mother.

On feet quick as a gazelle, Abby raced through the

castle. The silence inside magnified tenfold by the battle raging outside the stone walls. She thought she heard crying but knew her mother would not cry. She would fight. Abigail followed the sound up the stairwell into her very own chambers. It was not her mother, but her cousin, Agnes huddled in the corner looking frail. When Abigail stepped inside of the room, she saw the blood.

"Agnes, what have you done?"

"I am so sorry. I could not fend her off," Agnes cried.

She tried to wipe up the blood, but it seemed to be unstoppable. "I cannot lose you. You are more than my cousin; you are the sister of my heart."

"You must go to your mother and stop my own. She is bent on killing yours no matter the cost."

Abby rose quickly from where she had knelt beside her cousin and friend. "She is using blood magic? Your blood?" Gran would have called it her red-headed temper, but the just magic within her traveled to her center and filled her to overcome.

"I will not lose you, Agnes." With that promise, she ran out of her room, the power of Earth crying out, seeking her mother and her aunt.

Power pulsated from her fingertips. Abby ran through the castle looking for her mother. Her sixth sense told her she needed to hurry. The thought of losing her mother made it impossible to breathe, let alone think straight. She didn't know which way to turn when she arrived at the back stairwell. Should she climb up? Go out to the back gardens? Or, should she go down to the dungeons?

A commotion from her mother's private gardens made the choice for her. Abigail followed the sound of fighting. She heard her aunt shouting and deep inside knew all of this was because of Caitriona their lives were in peril.

"This should all be mine! He should be with me and not you. You cannot have everything Caoimhe. Give me the grimoire and I will let you live."

No. This cannot be happening. I cannot be too late. It was her nightmare come to life. Her aunt would kill her own sister if she did not intervene.

"You cannot kill me, sister. If you do, you will never find the grimoire. It does not answer your call. You have sold your soul and are no longer a Mórríganian."

"What I am is a powerful witch who gets what she wants. I've had the man who should have been mine."

"Aye, it took a spell of illusion for you to accomplish the deed for he would not bed one such as you if you had not used magic."

Abby finally had reached the garden gate; yet hesitated to enter. Could she truly be hearing the confession of her father's infidelity and her mother's knowledge of the same? Clearly it was a falsehood for her father was devoted to her mother.

Though the sounds of metal against metal continued. Horses whinnied, men shouted and the threat of war surrounded her, all she could do is stare at the two women whose magic enveloped them like a cocoon protecting a caterpillar. "Neither trusts the other," she whispered.

"Leave now, Caitriona. Go and call off your demon dogs of war and you will be unharmed. For I have tired of your tantrums and the abuse you have placed on my niece and my husband's child."

Abigail's gasp was covered by Caitriona's laughter. The cackle placed fear in the center of her being. Her aunt had yet to play her trump card. Which meant, she had been stalling and her mother was vulnerable. With her eyes closed, Abby released her own powers to search the growing wheat which stood tall and strong behind the Queen.

"Goodbye, Your Highness. Long live me," Caitriona laughed then flashed out of the garden.

"Mother, don't," she shouted. Bursting through the gate, Abby was sure she had warned her mother in time, but time is a tricky thing. It slows when you least expect it to. The sluggish way it teases you to believe it is on your side and then smacks you down into the mud like a servant who trips over buried deep rocks.

The creature was one she had never seen before. Surely, he was an upper-level demon for he had no horns, no distorted face or body. Truly he was as handsome as the dark power emanating from him. His form and his power tempted her. She feared her reaction. *It must be from my recent travels.*

"Witch," a voice sounded but his lips did not move. "Your book is my prize. Give it to me and I will keep you as my concubine."

"Go back to Hell, from whence you came, you foul beast," her mother shouted.

Abby watched as magically volley one after another was thrown at the creature to no avail. He continued his forward stride while her mother finally turned and ran into the wheat field.

Abby's heart pounded. She hid behind a large statue. Fear for herself and her mother kept her in place. What was this being that he could withstand the strongest witch of the age?

"Your fear is sweet and tempting, young one, but my mission is clear. Another time. Oh witch, is it games you like to play? Hmm? The young one smells so sweet. Is she yours? Should I play with her?"

"You leave her alone," Caoimhe shouted. Mother took the bait just as Abby knew she would. She had seen it in her vision. Now, she was no longer afraid. She knew what she had to do to try and save her mother. She ran into the wheatfield hoping what Orla, Gran and her mother had taught her would be enough.

"Give me what I want, witch." The demon had her mother by her throat. His eyes glowed red and claws protruded from former fingers.

"No."

"Then you will die."

"So mote it be."

Running away was not in her vernacular for the time being. As the demon struck, so did she. Tears ran freely as she watched her mother die at the hands of this animal. Dark magic met dark magic mixed with light as she combined spells once more.

"Rot in Hell where you belong." As it died, she fell to her knees taking in the remains of her mother's life-force and that of the demon's.

About the Authors

Hope Daniels

International Best Selling Author Hope Daniels grew up in a small resort area in Michigan where she and her husband still live today. As the third child of four, she had an exhaustive imagination. From straddling the back-porch railing as a wild cowgirl, to saving the world as Wonder Woman complete with homemade bullet stopping bracelets. She was always taking what she read and making it as real as she could, now if she could just find the wolf shifter of her dreams… Love of reading began at an early age, due to a first-grade teacher living next door, and her own father reading bible stories to her before bed each night. It was cemented in elementary when she discovered scholastic books, specifically Marguerite Henry's Misty of Chincoteague. Her love of horses and reading has never diminished, even after her husband took her to Chincoteague Island for their honeymoon. Daniels loves to write in

multiple genre which includes her short in the International Best Selling Anthology All You Need Is Love

produce by Encompass Ink titled Always and Forever, the Amazon Bestselling Anthology Black Magic (A

Women of Urban Fantasy Production), a Contemporary and YA short in the LDLInk Anthologies. She is

also the co-author to the Magical Forces series books Hell In Heels, Hell On The Heart, Hell Of A Family

Yule, Hell of A Night and Hell Is The Tie That Binds with Author Alicia Dawn. They expect to release The

Dragons Assassin with Lavish Publishing in 2021/22.

Alicia Dawn

Alicia Dawn is your average 9-5 workaholic that took care of every day business. After 10 long years of having no life, outside of home and work, she found Facebook as so many others had. Always having the passion, since she was in fourth grade, to read and write. She became captivated by all the stories others with the same reading and writing passion, created. Role Playing stories out on Facebook. Getting drawn into something that she had never done before, but always in back of her mind wished she could do, Alicia started Role Playing on Facebook in 2010, meeting Nikita Jakz, and Hope Daniels along the way. After a years, she decided to be adventurist and create her own characters. Not unlike what all authors do, when creating those awesome books that she had coveted and devoured when they came out. Today she continues to create and publish captivating adventures with her characters.

Also by HOPE DANIELS

A Love At Christmas

A Wylde River Beginnings

http://mybook.to/LoveatChristmas

Ruth Perry left Northern Ohio with her family knowing she would take the brunt of her stepfather's

wrath. James Delaney was happy to ride the range, farm, and take care of the family business along with

his brother Markus. On his way to Wylde River to report back, he spotted the auburn-haired beauty for

the first time. The Wylde River adventure begins with a family feud, but when love blooms between

Ruth and James, will their passion cost them everything?